The SHE You Don't See

ISBN: 978-1-7341346-2-9

LOC Control #: 2019918928

Publisher and Editor: Fiery Beacon Publishing House

(Fiery Beacon Consulting and Publishing Group)

Graphic Artist: Fiery Beacon Publishing House

This work was produced in Greensboro, North Carolina
United States of America.

The SHE You Don't See

By

Antonya Ballard

To My Grandparents

Wilbert and Queen Huntley......

This book is for you.

TABLE OF CONTENTS

The Introduction

How did you miss me? How did you not see? I was right there in front of you this entire time. But wait, that's not fair. I can't expect you to see my inner me if I'm blind to it myself. I mean, how could this be? How could I miss me? Every day I wake up and thank God because I'm alive and then I ask Him for forgiveness. Now before I ask God for anything, I begin to thank Him for who He is in my life. I thank Him for being my comforter, my friend, my way-maker and my provider. I could go on and on just giving Him thanks because truthfully, He's just that good. I begin to do as Romans 4:17 says, and call those things that are not, forth. I start rebuking every attack of the enemy then I roll over and see just how blessed I truly am. I am blessed to be married to my childhood sweetheart; it hasn't always been easy, but we survived. He loves God and puts his family first. We have anointed and talented kids, a beautiful home by the beach in L.A. and I'm the top neurologist in the country. Everybody's above the dirt and not below. Everybody has the use and activity of their limbs and are in their right minds. No one has been to jail or had any major surgeries. It's like my Pastor always says, nothing missing, nothing broken, needs are met, out of debt. Everything's the way they should be.

Beep! Beep! Beep! My alarm begins to ring; I lay there staring at the rays peeking through the drapes and think to myself, "What a beautiful Thursday morning this is!" I jump up, take a shower, and begin to beautify myself. I rush downstairs to cook breakfast and make everyone's favorite. I quickly begin to make grits, sausage, bacon, cheese eggs, pancakes, country ham, toast and freshly squeezed orange juice. I go to the stairs and yell to everyone, "Breakfast is ready!"

First comes Lisa - she was the baby girl. She was quiet, stayed to herself, very smart and was about to turn sixteen in three days. Next comes Jr.; he was our oldest son. He stood about 5 foot 7, very outgoing, athletic, seventeen and a spitting image of his father. As they entered into the kitchen, I greeted them. "Good morning my loves, have a wonderful day today!" I gave them a kiss and off to work I go. Laughing at the Steve Harvey morning show and singing as loud as I can, everything was going great. Seems good right? So again, I ask myself, how did I miss me? I mean what's missing; you look at my life and most would say I have everything, that I must be crazy and a part of me agrees; you're right - my family is together, and my career is at an all-time high. I am an upstanding member of the community and very active in my church. I live where I have always said I wanted to live and drive what I have always wanted to drive. Thank God we're not hurting financially but something's missing. What should make me smile, I frown and what should make me rejoice and be thankful, I cry and ask "why?" God, I'm not alone but why do I feel like I am? Anyone that knows me would automatically tell you, "oh she's loving, quiet, drama free, strong, intelligent, and most of all loves God. She's active in her community and church and very anointed," and yet, everyone only sees the outer me while I worry about the inner me that they don't see.

Chapter 1

The Beginning

I remember it like it was yesterday. I was sitting in my office curled up in front of the fireplace, wrapped up in my blanket and reading a very good book, and then I get to this quote by Vivek Thangaswamy that says:

"Being strong and positive is like holding your breathe under water - you will never be able to do it forever. Sometimes crying out and expressing yourself will help you from drowning."

I lean back, close my eyes and all of a sudden, I begin to cry and I'm not talking about small little tears but I began to whale. Lord, what's happening to me! Here I am crying uncontrollably, and everyone knows that's not me. I try to pull myself together because honestly, no one can see me like this, after all I'm Ranae. Yes, I cry but mostly in church. Now let me tell you, I'll go in for others. I love witnessing others receive their miracles and breakthroughs! I'll cry my lashes off and look drunk in the spirit; I'll even cry for my family, my children, my friends and especially my man. Truthfully, it doesn't really matter who it is because I'll cry if I see a homeless person outside and quickly run to assist. Everyone knows that I will support them, push them, and counsel them but hold on, because the "them" isn't here. It's just me. Then I hear this still small gentle voice say, "it's time Ranae." I quickly sat up and began to look around the room and didn't see anyone. I fell to my knees and begin to pray.

9

God you know I ain't ready yet. I begin to tell Him every reason why I thought I had to stay. I mean after all, my children need me, my husband needs me, my family, friends, job and the church need me. I'm too needed and there's a lot of things that I have to get right with you first before going anywhere. Just as I was about to go in, I hear that same small gentle voice say, "Your right everyone does need you, including Me. You ran great half full; now it's time for you to run whole. It's not time for you to go anywhere - it's time for you to be completely healed from the inside out. It's time for you to see what I see."

"What could you possibly see that I'm missing," I replied. "I pray every day, I read and study, take care of my home and try to help as many people as I can. I go to church and I'm always going or doing something for others. You said the greatest gift that we could give anybody is love and that is what I show on a daily basis." Then that gently voice replied, "your right Ranae', you do all those things and more and yet you're still running half full. You've spent so many years of your life covering, protecting and faking you, until you've totally pushed Me to the side. You're numb to life, numb to yourself and most of all numb to me. You believe that I can heal others, why can't you believe that I can do the same for you?"

Still sitting in my chair, this entire time I'm looking around the room because this voice is too loud, too sharp and too strong for me to be in this room alone. I sat back and said to myself, "Now you're tripping. Stop talking to yourself before someone comes down those stairs and think your just plum crazy and out of your mind." I sip some of my hot cocoa and attempt to read my book some more and then all of a sudden I hear that same gentle voice: "Ranae', why do you keep running from Me?" Ok, now either my husband or my kids have come down these steps and are playing with me. I jump up and begin to walk around the room, but no one was there - just me, my book and the fireplace. I sat back down and shook my head because I began to feel like Samuel in the bible. Very hesitant to answer, I replied, "How am I running when I'm working for you in kingdom?" The gentle voice then says, "And how is that - because you read and pray and go to church? A lot of people do that, and just like you, they do it in my name like I'm actually approving it. Yes, I have used you to witness to others, the testimonies are proof of that. My question though Ranae', is why do you choose to keep moving in my name illegally? So basically, what you're saying is, you care so much about other people and their feelings, life, breakthroughs, miracles and soul, to where you'd neglect your own?"

"No Lord," I said, "I care about me too. I'm not built for hell. I always tell you how I desire to make heaven my permanent home." The gentle voice replied, "Then let Me create in you a clean heart. These smiles and fake laughs that you've been giving people may fool them, but you already know it doesn't fool Me. You've hidden behind this mask saying, 'I don't need anyone but God; I'm ok and everything is fine and I can handle it and do all things through Christ by myself,' for so long, until you've become numb to your own true self. How can you truly attempt to help others if you're broken from the inside out? Ranae' it's time, let Me show you what I see."

Just as I was about to reply, the phone rang. "Whoo! Saved by the bell," I said. The conversation went a little something like this:

Them: Hello, Ranae' speaking? Girl, have you heard?

Me: Ummm… who is this?

Them: Ranae', this is Kimberly. Have you heard the news?

Me: What news?

Kimberly: Robert and Stacy are finally getting a divorce.

Dropping my head, I took a deep breath. "Lord," I said, "here we go." There's never a day that goes by where someone isn't calling or texting about some kind of problem. Lord, give me the strength for this one. Just as she was about to go into detail, the doorbell rang. I quickly begin to chuckle as I thought to myself, "God never lets me down and He's always on time." Saved by yet another bell, I said "Kim, I'll have to call you back because someone's at the door." I ran to the door and to my surprise it was Elder Veronica Tatum. Now Veronica is a whole beast by herself. She's an Elder of the church and always either in somebody's business or trying to call out everybody's sin, so this was an unexpected surprise. "How are you," I asked? She replied, "Oh I'm blessed and highly favored." Ok point taken – time to put on that fake smile. "Well come in. What brings you by?" I said. She takes a deep breath and says, "Ranae' we have a problem." Deeply concerned, I asked, "What's the problem?" She said, "Last Sunday another member of the church came to me about a personal family problem and I kind of messed up." "What do you mean kind of messed up," I asked. She began telling me about her conversation with Robert and Stacy and how she sort of let the conversation slip to someone else and now other people are finding out. "Ranae', what do I do? You know I've been praying to God to put a girdle on this tongue of mine but He hasn't answered that prayer yet." She went on to say, "I told them to come to me because I knew the Pastor was busy and Ranae', you already know I'm nosy." I replied sternly, "Veronica, it's like I tell you all the time - what people tell you in confidence should stay between you and them. It should never turn into a round table discussion with others. I mean, how would you feel if you confided in someone and they went and told your business to everyone else?" Elder replied, "Your right Ranae', I'm too old for this. I really believe I have a problem and I've been praying about it and I'm still waiting on that deliverance. I'm an Elder of the church and this is going to look bad. And oh my God, when Pastor hears about this, he's going to sit me down. Can he do that though? I'm a faithful tithe payer and I'm one of the founding members of the church. That should count for something right?" I look at her with the blank stare because truthfully, I was so confused. "So, Veronica, what your saying is, your more concerned about your title and being sat down more than running off at the mouth? Who cares that you're a faithful tithe payer or that you're one of the founding members; that doesn't give you an excuse to make others people's problems your topic of discussion. It's like Pastor tells us all the time, be mindful of your movement and your mouth and you, Veronica, always seem to do the opposite on both." Elder replied, "Well Ranae', maybe tomorrow when Pastor has altar call I'll go up there; who knows, this might be a job for the whole church because this demon keeps coming back. It's a stronghold Ranae." "Veronica," I said, "that's not a stronghold, that's your mouth and you have control over that. While you're here though, let's finish up on this report for Sunday." As we're sitting at the kitchen table going over the financial report for Sunday, that same small gentle voice came back yet again. "Ranae, see this is what I'm talking about; you quickly run to the aide of others or try to give advice but you're missing you and running from me."

"No I'm not," I replied, "I'm here but I don't understand." Then I noticed that Veronica was still sitting at the table just staring at me. "Ranae', are you ok," she asked. I quickly told her yes, but she didn't believe me. "No, you're not," she said. Of course I pretended to play it off and even asked for her to expound on her case. "Well for starters, you're talking to yourself. Now, I'm not the Pastor but you do know you can always come talk to me if you need to." I assured her that there was nothing to talk about and that I was just in deep thought and

14

starting speaking out loud. "Ranae', is it Damien?" I gave her this surprise look and asked, "why would it be my husband?" Elder replied, "Well everybody knows how much you two love each other but it's almost too good to be true." "We go through like everyone else; we just choose not to display our personal business in the company of others," I explained.

She then changed to the subject over to the kids. "You know children sometimes put their parents through a lot. Is it them," she asked? I looked at her for a good thirty seconds before answering. "Why would you think it's my children Veronica?" Ready with her response, she fired back, "because Ranae', no one's kids are perfect and you don't think we pay attention to you on Sunday's over there in that corner just crying and praying? Heck, most of us are trying to figure out if you're doing all that because of the spirit or if something's going on that you don't want anyone to know about. I sat back in my chair and said to her, "Veronica, this is what I'm talking about. Why are you and everyone else for that matter so concerned with what I have going on and not paying attention in the service? Why are you looking at me?" Veronica replied, "because our minds be wondering Ranae. But seriously, please know that I'm here for you whenever you want to talk." Trying to talk under my breathe I replied, "you and everyone else you mean." Elder heard me and quickly interjected, "Hey look Ranae', don't judge me. I'm praying about it." As we begin to finish up our report, Damien came down the steps.

Lovie, that's the nickname he gave me in high school and until this day he's never changed it. I heard him call me but there I sat, still surprised by Veronica. He calls again, "Lovie, I need your help if you don't mind. Oh, hello Elder Tatum, I didn't see you sitting there!", he said. Veronica spoke back and proceeded to ask him how everything was going. "Great! No complaints! How are you doing?" She prepared her answer ever so eloquently, "Oh I'm blessed and highly favored. So, Damien, did you hear about Robert and Stacy?" "Veronica," I yelled, "are you serious?" Here we go - now it's the devil's fault, right? With a matter-of-fact look on her face, she responded, "See Ranae, I told you it was a stronghold!" I shook my head and told her that I would just have to speak with her tomorrow in church. "Are you sure," she asked, "I mean, I can counsel you two right now if you want." Damien overheard and began asking questions. "Nothing. She was just about to leave." Damien replied, "Well, enjoy the rest of your evening Elder Tatum," as she prepared to leave. As I walked Elder to the door and closed it behind her, I turned around to a very displeasing look on Damien's face. "What's wrong," I asked? Damien replied sternly, "Ranae', please tell me you don't have people out here thinking we're having problems in our marriage?" I responded, "No, I promise I don't. It's a long story. What do you need help with?" He looked at me, then at the ground. He took a deep breath and begin to say, "Lovie, I've prayed long and hard before coming to you about anything and I'm certain this is the right decision to make." I prepared my heart and mind while he continued. "Things between us haven't always been easy, but personally, I think that over the years I've grown and matured and now I am a hard worker and I try my best to help provide for my family, would you agree?" Very curious and slow to answer I replied, "yes I agree Damien. You are a very hard worker I'll give you that. What's wrong?" "Well Ranae', how would you feel if I took a break for a while?"

Looking very confused I begin to ask, "what do you mean take a break?" He replied, "A break from being the head. I mean, you've held me and this family down plenty of times before. You held us down when I had nothing. When I couldn't make up my mind if I wanted to be in a relationship or marriage, you took care of the home, the kids, made sure that I had what I needed and made sure the bills were paid. You did your thing but truthfully, I'm tired. I've been thinking about this for a while now. I went and spoke to my boss on yesterday and quit my job. I just feel like I need about a year or two to get my thoughts together." "Damien," I yelled, "what do you mean get your thoughts together - we have a family, this house, bills and life!" Calmly he said, "Ranae' I know all of that and I wouldn't have done it if I felt like you wouldn't have been able to handle it. Outside of my mom, you're the next strongest woman I know. Trust me, I know you'll figure it out. I have no doubt in my mind. You say all the time that God will provide, so watch him do it now." He then kisses me on my forehead and says, "Love you honey," before running back upstairs. "What about how I feel about all of this," I yelled but he never answered.

Lord, what am I going to do? How am I going to handle all of this and especially on my own? This is a six-bedroom home, we have 2 luxury cars, kids, bills and life is still going on. The deep inner part of me wanted to cry so bad but the outer me wouldn't. I walked over to the mirror in the den and begin to tell myself, "Girl you got this! Solving problems, that's your specialty. You're used to paying bills and handling everything by yourself, you've got this!" Now why he felt that he needed a break is beyond me; I couldn't figure that one out at all. "A break from what," I asked myself? I'm not even going to let this stress me out. I can't. This is just another problem I need to fix. Everything's going to be ok.

Chapter 2

When the Breaking Begins

As I turned to go back into my office and attempt to finish reading my book the phone begins to ring. Very reluctant to answer, "Hello," I said, "Ranae' speaking." The response came through frantically: "Ranae', we need you to get to the hospital as fast as you can; it's Lamar and it's not looking good. Now Lamar was every bit of 6 foot 4 and weighed about 230 pounds. He was loved by many and hated by some. He was a family man but more importantly he loved God. He loved his wife and kids and would do anything for them, and everyone knew if you messed with his family or his money, he was coming for you. He was a great cook and the best male dresser at the church. He had the voice of an angel and would put you in check real quick if he needed to. He was a friend, a protector and most of all, my uncle. He was the father I never had. He took me to live with him and his family at a very young age. I yelled upstairs, "Damien, we have to get to the hospital now, it's Lamar, please we have to hurry. "

As we begin to drive to the hospital, Damien looks over at me and says, "Lovie, we really need to stop for gas before going or we won't make it and I don't have any money on me right now." "Fine," I replied, "I can't think about this right now, just do what you have to do so we can get there please." We pulled up to the hospital and got out of the car. Once inside, we were stopped by my cousin, Jamie. Now Jamie was a handful. She was my uncle's youngest daughter and the one that would get you told in a minute. "Ranae'," she says, "You're too late. He's gone. "No," I screamed! I fell to my knees thinking that this couldn't be right! God, he can't be gone! Damien runs over, grabs me by my arms and sits me in a chair. The inner me wanted to scream out so loudly, but the outer me wouldn't. I became completely numb and was at a loss for words. As I sat there in a daze, the entire family came downstairs. Everyone began asking me if I was alright, but nothing would come out. Then I hear my aunt Loula-Mae burst out, "That's Ranae ya'll! Of course she's hurt! That man was like a father to her but she's as tough as nails. She's going to be alright. Just make sure she handles everything because you already know if she handles it, it'll be done right." In my head I began thinking, "I don't want to handle anything. I just want to run so far away from everything and everybody," but nothing would come out. I looked over at Damien and asked him to take me home.

The drive that should have only taken about 25 minutes seemed like it took forever. As I gazed out the window with tears in my eyes, Damien grabs my hand. "Ranae', I'm really sorry about Lamar. You know he loved you like his own daughter. Look I know this isn't the right time to talk about this but truthfully, there's never going to be a good time. Not only am I wanting to take a break from being the head in our home but I'm also needing a break from our marriage." I snatch my hand away as fast as I could, looked at him and said, "Wait a minute! Really? I mean really?? You're going to do this now?" Damien replied, "Look I'm sorry Ranae' but I have to get this out. It's not you. I already know it's me. You do everything a wife should and more. But me personally, I'm not happy. I mean, I love the fact that you're a strong, independent woman but sometimes I feel like you don't need me. Let a problem arise, and you're already on top of it. Most of the time, I find out things after it's already been handled. Not only that, but I'm tired of being tied down. I want to be able to date more than one woman if I choose to. God only gave us one life to live and I know for a fact that He wants me to be happy in it; He wants me to make the most of my life. I've tried the being faithful to one woman thing, and that's not working for me. I tried to be the husband that you deserve but deep down all I'm doing is lying to you and our children and most importantly myself, so I've decided no more lies. I'm going to be me and do me. I know you'll be fine. I've also decided that I want to move out of the house by the end of the week. Now don't worry because most of the things in the house belong to you. I already know that I was going to stop working so I won't try to fight you for anything."

Just as I was about to give him a piece of my mind, we pulled in the driveway and immediately saw our children running out to greet us. I put my head down because I was too ashamed to look them in their faces and tell them the family they've always known was about to break apart and if that wasn't bad enough, their favorite uncle had just passed. "Hey dad what's up?" Damien looks at them both and said, "I really need you guys to give your mother your undivided attention. She has something very important to go over with you and I need you to pay close attention. I looked at him with a mean mug face because I couldn't believe this man would put all of this on me to handle after everything that just happened. I shook my head, slammed the car door, ran in the house, went upstairs and locked myself in my room. I dropped to my knees and cried out, "Lord, why is this happening to me and all at once?" As I laid on the floor face down praying, I got this loud knock on the door. "Mom, it's Lisa, are you ok?" Pulling all of the strength that I could muster up I said, "Yes I am baby; I'll be out just give me a minute." My children had never seen me like that before. I always seem to have it together in front of them. I began telling myself, "You don't have time to sit and have a pity party right now. You have to pull yourself together. It's too many people who are needing and depending on you."

Just as I begin to get up off the floor, I get another loud knock on the door. "Lisa, I told you I'll be out in a minute." "Girl, this ain't Lisa" the voice replied, "It's Traci. Get out here, I need to talk to you now, it's an emergency!" Oh God, I said, not her. Why is she here; this isn't the right time. Traci was my half-sister on my real daddy's side and always needing money or some kind of advice. I opened the door and asked, "what is it Traci?" As I expected, she confirmed my thoughts: "Ranae' we

22

have to talk. I need your help." With everything else that had transpired, I didn't have the strength to face the conversation. "Traci this isn't a good time. I have a lot going on right now and Lamar just passed. So can this just wait?" "Oh wow," she replied, "I'm so sorry to hear that. My prayers are with you and the family seriously. But for real, no, this can't wait. I need your help! Don't ask me how, but I am three months late on my rent. Normally they give me time to pay it but they won't do it this time. They said if I don't come up with $4,000.00 by 5pm this afternoon, they are padlocking my doors and me and the kids will have nowhere to go. So, I need about $4000.00 if you don't mind or you could just let me and the kids move in here with you; I promise I won't be any trouble."

As I lifted up my head, I looked her in her eyes and asked, "why are my thoughts and feelings never taken into consideration? Why am I always overlooked like it's ok and like I'm some strong superwoman who never hurts, cries, or have bad days?" "Ranae'", she quickly says, "you know if it wasn't a true emergency, I wouldn't be coming to you. I mean it's been four months since I've asked you for anything. I've been doing good and if it's the money, I'll pay you back. Now you know I can't pay it back all at once, but it will get done little by little." The day's events felt like a nightmare and this conversation didn't help. "Look! I don't care Traci. I'm just mentally tired." I pushed passed her, ran downstairs, picked up my car keys, jumped in the car and headed straight for the beach.

Chapter 3

It's Time to See What I See

One good thing about where we lived is that it was only about ten minutes from the beach and any time I needed to get away, that's where I'd go. It's something about sitting there staring out at the water and thinking. As I drove down the strip of the beach I screamed, "God! What did I do to deserve any of this? This is way too much for me to handle right now. I mean you said in your Word that you wouldn't give us any more than we could bear, and this is way too much." I parked the car, got out and walked onto the sand. I laid out my beach towel, sat down with my bible in my hand and begin to stare out at the water. I closed my eyes, and begin to tell myself, "Ranae', this is just another hurdle that you have to jump over. You're tough and this is not going to kill you. Yes you're down but you're going to be fine! You've got this." Just as I was about to take a deep breath, I hear that small, gently voice yet again, "Ranae' do I have your attention now? Are you ready to face you and see what I see?" "Yes," I replied, "what am I missing?" Then all of a sudden, I was lifted up off the beach towel and found myself in my old room.

What is this? Why am I here? I left this place when I was fourteen years old. "Yes I know," the gentle voice replied. "You've been running ever since. Just watch and pay close attention." Standing there looking at this room brought back so many memories. I had a small room with no windows. It had no dressers, television or bed, just 4 walls and a little closet for my few cloths and shoes. I saw this little girl walk in, laid on the floor and began to pray. "God," she says, "You made me so that means You love me right, but I don't understand - how could You love me and allow this to happen to me? After all, I'm only a child. My parents have been abusing me ever since I can remember. My dad is more consumed with his image than being my dad and my mom doesn't even want me to exist. I've been raped way too many times to count and beaten because I say I'm hungry. I've slept in abandoned cars and rundown houses just to try to escape my life here. I've even tried to kill myself but that didn't work either. It's been five days now since I've eaten anything, but uncle Lamar keeps telling me to keep the faith, that you're not going to leave me or forsake me, that you have my back and you're going to help me. Well, I kind of need your help now because I don't know what else to do. I save my lunch from school just so I can have something later on when I get hungry at home. I constantly yell out, 'Lord help,' and I hear nothing. Please forgive me if I'm being selfish. I mean after all, You have this whole world to look after and I know You're probably off helping someone who is way worse off than me but, can you please just add me to your list of people to help? I'm trying to keep the faith and stand strong but it's getting a little hard. Well God, I need to wrap this prayer up because if they find me praying, it's going to be a beating for me, but please know that I love you. And oh, let me tell you what I've been thinking. Only because I know your busy and all, I thought I would help you out some. So, because the people that I know are crazy at times and very hurtful, I've decided to build this imaginary glass wall, and everyone who hurts me or does something hurtful to me will go behind that wall. This wall will be there to protect my feelings and keep me from getting hurt. What do you think God? Well, I love you. And I'll come and talk to you later on tonight. And please if you can, let uncle Lamar stop by tonight and visit me. That's the only time I get to feel loved and important."

As I stood there watching and listening to the prayer, all I could do was cry because I remembered that day. I was just coming in from school and I wanted to pray before my parents got home. God did answer the prayer about uncle Lamar coming over. He came over that night with a McDonald's happy meal and a big bag of potato chips. He brought me a bible and told me to read it every night and to remember that Jesus loved me and that no matter what it looked like or how it felt, God was always there for me.

The gentle voice asked, "What else do you remember about that night Ranae?" "Everything," I replied. "I remember after that prayer I got up and opened the door and was immediately smacked in the face." I could hear it clear as day: "Why isn't this house cleaned like I told you Ranae'? "I'm sorry mama," I replied. I'll get to it now. I was finishing up my homework." My mom's voice drowned out my reasoning and

27

was followed up with, "I don't care what you were doing just do what I told you to do before I take my fist and knock you under that table." Walking over to get the broom I quietly said, "yes ma'am." I was only twelve at the time and I could remember it just like it was yesterday. Before Uncle Lamar came to visit, my parents decided to have some friends over. I went to my room because I didn't want to be around all that smoke. Then I heard my mom yelling my name. "Ranae' get your butt out here now."

I came running down the hallway until she told me to stop and turn around. I begin to cry because I knew where this was heading. She started the bidding off at $25.00. My mom sold me to one of her male friends for $150.00 that night. "Mom please! I don't want to." She replied with, "girl shut up and be thankful. You just paid the light bill. See I've always told you that you were blessed. Every month we receive a blessing because of you. Now go do what you're supposed to do." I never knew their names, but this one picked me up and took me in the room and shut the door. So many feelings came upon me that night. The feeling of guilt, shame, low self-esteem, unworthiness, ugliness, depression and that I would never amount to anything just to name a few. "God," I asked, "why am I here?" I haven't thought about this in a long time." "Yes, I know," the gentle voice replied, "just keep watching." The little girl came out of the guest room with tears in her eyes, ran to her bedroom and fell on the floor saying, "this is going behind the glass wall. All of those feelings that came upon me that night, I told myself, would go behind the glass wall and never again would I allow this or these feelings to hurt me; this is only going to make me tougher and stronger. One day I'm going to be older and I'm running as far away from this place as I possibly can. I'm going make something of myself and have a great life and kids of my own. So nope, I'm not going to keep crying over this, I'm going to sleep and get ready for whatever tomorrow holds. I'm Ranae', and I can handle anything that comes my way, I got this!" She went in the bathroom and took a long, hot shower, came out and went straight to bed. As I continued to relive my past, I realized that I had never dealt with any of those issues that attached itself to me that night - I just placed them behind a wall.

Standing there bent over trying to catch my breath, the gentle voice said, "Breath Renae! What's wrong?" "What's wrong," I replied, "everything is wrong. I buried these thoughts and feelings a long time ago. I vowed to never think about them again. I didn't want to see this. Why am I here?" The gentle voice continued to say, "because I need you to see what I see. You built that glass wall which means you hardened your heart. Everything that hurt you or you thought would hurt you went behind it. Not one time did you give any of it to Me. You immediately begin making plans for your own life and future. Jeremiah 29:11 says, 'For I know the plans I have for you, declares the Lord, plans to prosper you and not to harm you, plans to give you hope and a future.' You asked for My help but you had already made up in your mind what you were going to do. You never gave me a chance to do anything. You quit having faith in me."

"No I didn't," I replied, "I had faith in you!" The gentle voice then asked me a question, "Ranae' faith comes by what?" As if the passage had been embedded in my heart, I replied, "Your right." The gentle voice confirmed, "but look at what you've been hearing all these years? All you've been hearing is I, I, I. I'm Ranae', I got this, I can handle this. I don't need anybody. I'll make it happen. Your faith began to grow in you and what you thought you could do for yourself more than Me. Proverbs 3:5-6 says, Trust in the Lord with all of your heart, and lean not to your own understanding; In all your ways acknowledge Him, And He shall direct your path. Your trust was in you and what you wanted and your own understanding you began to map out and plan your own paths for life. If it didn't feel or look right to you, or happen in your timing, it went behind the glass wall. You became your own god. You lost faith in Me."

"But I was only a little girl," I begin to say, "I tried to have faith. Uncle Lamar would come and take me to church, and everyone would always tell me to keep the faith and I did. I kept believing in You but you never answered me. I felt like I had to do something. The gentle voice said, "again listen to yourself Ranae. You felt like you had to do something because I never answered you so you decided to become the god in your life and take over. Not one time did you stop to think how much that hurt me. Yes you would pray to me, but you didn't believe in any of it. You gave lip action, and you taught yourself to become an emotional being.

"What do you mean," I asked. The gentle voice went on to say, "As you grew older, you came to me on your timing. You stopped trying to develop a true relationship with Me. When life became too hard, yes you would pray and in your mind you wanted Me to move but truthfully in your heart, you didn't really care if I was going to move or not, because you already knew what you were going to do. You had already figured it out on your own. Do you know how hurtful it was to watch you go to church Sunday after Sunday and leave the same way you came in? You would get all dressed up, you would pray, shout and call on Me for everyone else but yourself. You became an emotional being. You taught yourself how to fake your true feelings so well outside of church, until you begin to bring it into church, and what's worse, you never once realized what you were doing. I mean you were the great Ranae and no one could tell you anything different. From your heart you wanted Me to move for others, but when I wanted to move for you; all you would do was cry and instead of giving me your heart and your issues, you immediately begin to try to worship Me from your mind which is impossible. You prayed when you wanted, you fasted when you wanted, you gave praise when you wanted, you worshipped when you wanted, but your heart wasn't there Ranae. John 4:24

says, 'God is spirit, and those who worship Him must worship in spirit and truth', and you had neither spirit nor truth.

Then all of a sudden, the gentle voice stopped speaking and I was all alone. "Oh God, what have I done," I begin to say. I dropped to my knees and began to plead my case: "I never asked for any of this! I was only a child. I didn't know what else to do. I wanted help. I was tired. All I wanted was to be loved. All I wanted was to feel like I belonged. All I wanted was to feel important. All I wanted was to feel beautiful. Every time a man touched me he stripped a piece away from me. Every time I was hit, it took a piece from me. I didn't know what else to do and I was tired of hurting. I was tired of praying to a God that seemed like He didn't care about me either. You never answered me. You never stopped those men from raping me. You never stopped my parents from beating on me. Every time I decided to do everybody a favor and kill myself You never didn't change my mind. As a matter of fact, You allowed me to try a few times, though I didn't succeed. If you really cared about me, and loved me, why would you let me continue to go through that? What did I ever do to deserve any of that? I'm sorry but I felt like I had to do something to protect me!"

Chapter 4

How Did I Get to this Point?

All of a sudden, I blinked my eyes and could not believe
where I ended up next, outside of Lamar's house. Lamar got
tired of me fending for myself, and fighting off men, and going
days without eating, so he came and took me from my parents
and moved me in with him and his family. I only got along with
his daughter Jamie; everyone else hated me and I never
understood why. I was happy that he brought me to live with
him. I mean after all I ate every day and had more clothes and
shoes to wear. He really treated me as if I was one of his own
daughters. He would always tell me that God had a calling on
my life and that he could not explain it but God would not let
him abandon me. He would always tell me that he believed he
was the guardian angel assigned to my life and that he was
determined to make sure that I knew God for myself. He would
read the bible with me, take me to church and pray with me. He
would always say, "Ranae' you have to know God for yourself.
You can't just go off what I say. You have to invite Him into
your life so He can protect, lead and guide you." I loved how he
made sure that I not only knew who God was, but he made sure
that I knew who I was. I could not tell him that I was down or
depressed or that I thought I was ugly or worthless. Lamar would
always come back and say, "God created you in His image
Ranae and when He created you, He didn't just throw you

together but instead, took His time and carefully planned out every detail to the T." He would tell me, "No, you didn't ask for the life you were given, but it was given to you because He equipped you to handle it. Everything happens for a reason and purpose - one day you will realize what that purpose is." Though he loved me, his wife hated me for it. My aunt Loula-Mae was my mom's youngest sister and she and Lamar would always get into arguments over me being there. I could remember telling him one day, "I'll leave because I don't want to be a bother to you," but he refused and reassured me that I was family.

As I am standing there looking at my past, the gentle voice said, "This is what I wanted you to see so pay close attention." I saw little Ranae' come in from school; she went straight to the kitchen to get a snack. "And what do you think you're doing little girl?", Aunt Loula-Mae asked. "I'm sorry," I replied, "I was hungry and thought I would fix something to eat." She snapped back, "and what money do you put in this house? I don't even know why your uncle brought you here. I told him your family problems are not our problems. The apple doesn't fall far from the tree. You're going to end up following right in the footsteps of one of your ungrateful parents." "No, I'm not" I replied, she then smacked me in the face and said, "you better not talk back to me girl because that's the quickest way to get yourself put out this house." "Yes ma'am," I replied. It was in that moment, the feeling of being unloved, and unwanted, confused and just flat out tired of being mistreated for no reason quickly came upon me. I picked up my bookbag and as I was heading to my room, I begin to tell myself, I'm not going to cry; I will show her that I am nothing like either of my parents and these feelings and my aunt will be something else that will go behind the glass wall. As I stood there with tears in my eyes, I realized that it was in that moment my trust in people had completely vanished and I realized that I would say that I loved people, but I had stopped wanted to be around them.

I never grew up with close friends, I completely pulled away from my family and begin to distance myself from everyone. I begin to view the world with just me in it. I became a loner and I never dealt with those issues. Standing there with my head down, mentally all I could ask myself was "what did I do?" It felt like everything had paused in that moment and when I lifted my head, it felt like the horrible movie resumed. It picked up with me laying on the bed, and I hear a knock at the door. "Ranae, it's me Lamar, can I come in please?" "Sure," I said. He came in and sat on the bed and begin to say, "you know you're always welcomed here; your aunt is just not willing to open up her heart, but you don't let this get you down." I looked at him with tears in my eyes and begin to say, "I'm not. I built this wall around my heart when I lived with my parents," I begin to tell him. "Any painful feelings that I begin to feel or anyone that hurts me or I think will hurt me, automatically goes behind it." He said, "ummm... tell me some more about this wall; what is its purpose?" I began to tell him, "It's purpose is to keep hurt away from me. Nothing or no one is ever going to get that close to me again to hurt me." After listening to what I had to say, Uncle Lamar stood up and walked over to the window. He just stood there gazing at the sky and was quiet for what felt like eternity. He looked back at me with tears in his eyes and asked, "why would you do that?" I replied, "Because people are cruel and crazy." "Ranae," he said, "Trust me when I tell you, that's not something you want to do. There's so much wrong in doing that. What you need to do is give it to God and let Him work things out on your behalf; He knows what's best. 1 Peter 5:7 says 'Cast all of your cares upon Him because He cares for you'. Don't try to take life on by yourself. You need God in your life.

I sat up in the bed and begin to stare at the ground. I took a deep breath and let it out because deep down I knew within my heart that my uncle was telling me the truth, but I didn't want to listen, didn't know what to say, and most of all, I didn't want to tell him that he was right. Sitting there staring at the ground and trying to think of something to come back with, all I could say was, "Oh uncle, I have God in my life. I'll never forget about Him; He will always be there, and I will always keep Him first but He's busy with all the other people in the world, so I decided to help Him out a little. I'll keep telling Him my problems because that's what I'm supposed to do but He won't mind my help." Uncle Lamar looked with tears streaming down his face and said, "Ranae, your headed for a life of destruction. You've hardened your heart to people and life, and mark my words child, one day this glass wall of yours is going to break and I just hope and pray that you're able to handle all those feelings that you've never dealt with and the people that you've stored up for so long behind it." "Oh Lamar," I said, "trust me, this is a strong wall. You taught me to have faith, right? I have faith that this wall is never going to break and that this wall will forever be here to do what I need it to do." He kissed me on my forehead and walked out the room. I heard him go to his room which was right beside mine, shut the door and he immediately begin praying. I heard him begin to ask God to forgive me, to shield and protect me and cover me under His blood. I mean my uncle begin to go forth hard on my behalf. I got up and shut my door and looked towards Heaven and said, "God, don't worry. We got this."

All of a sudden I begin to hear that gentle small voice, "Ranae, you see, I was always with you. You said I didn't care but I did. No I didn't come down physically and sit right beside you but I sent people in your life to speak on my behalf. Your uncle was filled with my spirit; he always spoke positive words into your life. He never let you forget who I was. You had questions and he had answers but you would never listen to him. You wanted to feel loved, so he gave that to you and reminded you of My love for you. When you wanted to feel important, he gave that to you and would remind you of how important you were to me. You wanted to feel beautiful and he would tell you that you were constantly; he would remind you that I created you in My image. You wanted to kill yourself, yes you tried, but you're right, it didn't work because I have plans for you. You thought what you went through was only for you? Oh dear child, it's so much bigger than you realize.

You forgot, I knew you way before you were ever a thought in the earthly realm. You didn't think that I already knew you were going to go through this? Listen, My only son came down from His thrown to redeem man back to Me. From the moment He got here, He was an outcast. Do you remember reading about King Herod? He wanted my son dead from birth, and He hadn't done anything to deserve that. You don't think it hurt My heart to see how he was treated? You have children Ranae - can you imagine the pain that I as a Father must have felt to watch My only son go through all that cruelty? He was part divine and yet part human. Do you not think that His flesh didn't hurt, that He didn't cry even at times or that His heart didn't ache? I mean after all, everyone tends to forget that a part of Him was actually human. He felt pain and hurt; He knew what it felt like to feel completely alone and yet He still chose to go through all of that for you because He loves you that much. I could have saved Him a few times; actually, He could have saved Himself because remember, He was also part divine, but He chose not to, because He knew that it was way bigger than Him.

"Do you recall," the gentle voice said, "when He prayed to me and asked that the cup would pass? Can you imagine how he felt in that moment knowing what was about to happen to Him? He loved you all so much that he endured it anyway and knew what it felt like to be betrayed by those closest to Him. Do you remember reading about the men that were with Him in the garden and they were supposed to pray with Him, but they kept going to sleep? Can you imagine how He must have felt in the moments that they were supposed to be covering Him? He was betrayed by a kiss, not a word but an action. Ranae, let me ask you something: knowing that a kiss is a gesture to show an outward expressing of love, or desire, how do you think that made Him feel? This was done by someone that was close to Him - someone that He loved and covered and taught and poured into and he was betrayed for money! Then, to know that someone else whom He was close to and shared things with and poured into and fasted for and loved would deny Him not once but three times out of what, fear? Can you imagine how I felt to see that as a Father and how my Son felt? He took on the sins of the world and for a moment even felt like I, His Father, deserted Him when he hung there on the cross.

How do you think I feel when I think back on everything that My Son went through to save and redeem man back to Me only to see them take matters into their own hands, forget about Me and the sacrifice that Jesus made, do what they want to do when they want to do it and even play with me like I'm a joke.

He endured all of that so you wouldn't have to. And yet, you chose to endure it anyway. I've always been there and never left your side. I placed a gift inside of you a very long time ago and the enemy knew it. He never wanted you to find out what it was. Everyone has a gift on the inside of them that's way bigger than their carnal minds could ever imagine. Remember John 14:12 when it says,

'Verily, verily, I say unto you, He that believeth on me, the works that I do shall he do also; and greater works than these shall he do; because I go unto my Father'.

Some have tapped into and discovered their gifts, but there's still a lot of people who are searching and if they would only come to Me, I could help them." The gentle voice continued, "I'll never make anyone serve me. Everyone has a choice. I want you to make the choice in your heart to let me in. Tear down this wall Ranae, I need you to for kingdom. There are so many people that need you. Yes you've been through a lot but I've allowed you to survive it all. You may have come out with scars, but scars heal. Let Me heal you. Let Me clean you from the inside out. Yes you made it out. You went to school, you obtained a degree, you had two beautiful children and married your high school sweetheart, not because that's who I had for you but because that was yet another situation that you could control. When people look at you, they see the outer you. Ranae', the great. She smiles, prays and is financially stable! Ranae' is loved and called upon by many; she's a fixer, quiet, humble, a hard worker, loves God, and teaches others to love and give it all to God. She loves and will do anything for her family - she covers, she's a giver, she has a big heart, there's not much that she doesn't know how to do and if she doesn't know how to do something she'll learn and do it herself. Renae', the super woman, is not a procrastinator - she's a mover! The list is endless, but you're broken on the inside and that's what I want to deal with Ranae. And even though you chose to leave Me and build your own god within yourself, I still was by your side."

The heart to heart conversation continued, "Do you realize that My hand of protection was on you this entire time? You think that all you have is because of your own strength? Everything you have because I allowed it! Even though you didn't deserve it, I still allowed it because I love you that much. I need you. Let me show you what life would have been like without My hand covering you."

Chapter 5

When the Healing Begins

The gentle voice was quiet, and I can't really explain the feeling that came over me but I felt so alone and cold. I felt empty, and life begin to flash before my eyes as I began to see my life turn in many different directions. One moment, I saw myself selling my body for drugs to pay my bills. I saw myself being pimped out. I saw myself being beat beyond recognition and being raped by males and females. Then, I saw myself behind bars for killing my parents and every man that every touched me; I didn't care about my life or anyone in it. I felt every feeling as if it were actually happening to me. Every pain, every heart ache, every needle going into my arm, every rape - my flesh felt it all. I dropped to my knees and begin to yell out, "Please God, I can't see this anymore. I can't feel this anymore. Please make it stop!"

I began to see myself hurting so many innocent people; manipulating situations and people's hearts because I didn't care at all. I could see people sitting and hurting and crying because I inflicted the same pain on them that I endured; I showed them the kind of love that I received and that was the worse feeling. He let me feel the hurt and pain from all of those people. "Please God," I kept yelling, "I can't take this!" Then I saw myself laying in a bathtub dead because I had cut my wrists. The gentle voice then said, "Ranae, this is just a sample of how your life could have turned out, but it didn't because of My love for you. If you really want to see Me, then you have to tear down this wall. You won't enter into my kingdom still holding on to all of this. Remember John 10:10 says,

'The thief cometh not, but for to steal, and to kill, and to destroy, but I am come that they might have life, and that they might have it more abundantly.'

You have let the enemy play on your mind long enough, and when someone steals something that means they have taken it without permission with no intent to give it back. Trust Me when I tell you Ranae, the enemy can't do any more than you allow Him to do. You've allowed him to steal your joy, your happiness, your peace, your self-worth long enough. You've allowed him to play on your mind long enough; it's time to fight back. You walk around like you control your life. You walk around like you hold your destiny and as if you're promised tomorrow; that's so far from the truth. Every morning you wake up, is a gift. Every breath you take, is a gift. Every step you take, is a gift. It's time to fight and take back what's yours, but as long as you keep pretending with yourself and others, you'll never be free. My son died so that you may have a right to the tree of life. He conquered hell and the grave, for you. He loves you so much and pleads on your behalf all the time."

The gentle whisper continued to impart to my soul: "Close your eyes Ranae and imagine this: the enemy coming to me every

44

day trying to convince me that I should just turn you over to him, because you don't love Me as much as I love you. He throws in my face how you do things on your own and don't even think about Me until it's something that's too big for you to handle. He constantly throws in My face how it was a mistake to allow you to get this far and that you'll never change. If that's not hurtful enough, he then begins to throw up how you go to church and just play and play like I'm a joke. He tells me every reason why I should just give you up to him, but My Son says, 'but Father, she really loves you deep down. Yes, she's lost right now, but don't give up on her. I know she will make the right decision. I know that she will choose within her heart to serve you and only you.' He pleads your case Ranae, because of His love for you and He's repaid by this wall of yours?"

"Oh God," I begin to scream out, "please help me. I don't know how to let this go. There are years and years of pain and people behind this wall. What do I do, where do I begin?" And in a blink of an eye, I was sitting on my beach towel looking out at the water. I quickly jumped up with tears in my eyes, ran to my car and begin to drive home. As I pulled in the driveway I noticed that Damien was putting his cloths into his car. I ran up to him gave him the biggest hug and said, "I forgive you and most of all I pray that you can forgive me. I release you." I ran in the house and called for my kids. Jr., Lisa. "I need to see both of you right away," I begin to yell. "Mom, where were you? I was so worried," Lisa begin to say, as she was running down the stairs. "Yes mom," Jr. replied!

"I want to apologize to you both I begin to say. I've called myself trying to shelter both of you from life and hurt for so long. I helped create this illusion of what life should look like and feel like and that wasn't fair to either of you. God blessed me with two of His angels and I mishandled both of you because of my past hurt and pain; I decided within myself to create a life for you both that was full of what I thought was love and what I thought should look like and feel like. That wasn't fair to either of you. I taught both of you to never let anyone tell you what you couldn't do and what you couldn't be and to always make them a lie. I taught both of you to hide your feelings and never show hurt or pain and to always do things for yourself. While most of it was done with good intent, I never taught you that you needed God in your lives for real.

I taught you to depend on yourself and not God. You may have gone to church with me, but I taught you how to fake it. I taught you how to be emotional beings and that was wrong. I was supposed to train you guys in the right way and I failed you both. I gave you what I knew and what I created for myself. There's no shame in showing your true feelings. It's when you're truthful with yourself and with God that he can truly move in your life. I know that both of you have feelings right now because of the emotional stress that you've seen me and your father go through and what I've been through with family and friends, but that's not your cross to bear; you both need to let it go and give it to God. Let him heal you and work out whatever the situation is. He's the only one that can fix it. I don't want either of you to learn the hard way like I did. The generational curse breaks today. I pulled both of them close, gave them a kiss and said, "I love you both. I need you both but most importantly God needs you and change starts today."

They both look at me with tears in their eyes because they had never seen me express anything for myself before. "Mom," Jr. says, thank you. For so long I have told God that I needed to protect you. I stopped being a kid because I needed to be a man and cover my mom and her feelings and that was a lot on me. It was a lot to see you go through so much with me not being able to do anything about it because I was too young, so thank you because this is a burden that has been lifted off of me. Thank you, mom, for releasing me." All I could do was drop to my knees and cry.

Lisa, knelt down, wrapped her arm around me and begin to said "Mom, I have something to tell you." "What is it baby," I asked? "I remember when I was very young and you told me that I was a blessing to you because you didn't really want me but I was a miracle child. Do you remember telling me that you tried to have an abortion with me but it wouldn't go through? That stuck with me all these years and I told myself at a very young age that if my mom tried to kill me but it didn't happen it was because God wanted me here for her. Since then, I have felt every pain you've felt. Do you recall how much I would stay under you? Do you recall me trying to give you advice even at a young age? It was because God told me that I needed to be strength for my mom. God came to me in a dream and told me that I needed to cover you in prayer. And there were many days that I would go off to myself and just pray to God for you. Thank you mom, for finally listening to God. Thank you for releasing me, and mom, I don't know what this means, but God is telling me to tell you that it's time to release everyone." I quickly looked up at her and said "Lisa, thank you." I looked towards heaven and said "God, even my kids were covering me, when I should have been covering them."

Chapter 6

When You Leave in Victory

The next morning, I woke up bright and early, went downstairs and begin to cook breakfast. Damien still left the house but I yelled up the stairs and called for Jr and Lisa. "Kids, it's time to wake up! It's Sunday and we have to get ready for church; breakfast is ready!", I yelled. I felt so good in my spirit. I got up, took my shower, and made pancakes, bacon, cheese eggs, grits, country ham, biscuits and gravy, oatmeal, fruit and fresh home-made apple juice. The kids came down, I fixed their plates and we all sat at the table and ate together. As we were sitting there eating, Jr. looks up and says, "mom, we haven't done this in a long time, thank you." That put the biggest smile on my face. We sat there happy for the first time in a long time just being ourselves, eating, laughing, and talking.

"Ok kids," I begin to say. "It's time to go upstairs and get ready for church." As I begin to clean up the kitchen, I cut on my Pandora and went in singing, moving about in complete joy. I can't even begin to describe the feeling that came over me. Now my church wasn't perfect but no church is. We had our challenges but we were a family. I've been a faithful member of For His Glory Non-Denominational Church for the past 18 years. The church was under the leadership of Sr. Pastor and Founder, Bishop C.V. Grain and First Lady Grain. As we pulled in the parking lot we could hear the music playing. To me, we had the best musical department in L.A.

We went inside and were immediately greeted by Elder Tatum. Ranae; she said, "where have you been? I've been calling and texting you. We need to talk before service starts." Standing with Jr. and Lisa by my side, I look at her and say, "not now Veronica." She quickly realizes that Damien wasn't with us. "Hey Ranae," she said, "Where's Damien? Is he working today?" I just looked at her and smiled and said, "Veronica, I release you and I love you." Sitting there with my children by my side was the best feeling ever.

Praise and worship was so uplifting. Every song had purpose and meaning. I promised God that when I went into the church, that I, me, Ranae refused to leave the same way, and if that meant being selfish for a moment, so be it. As I stood there with tears running down my face, I closed my eyes and said, "God, I give all of it to you." The praise team was singing a song by Tasha Cobbs-Leonard, entitled "Heart of Worship". "God," I begin to say, "I don't want it anymore. Please help me," and at that moment, something broke within me. I felt pain, shame, loneliness, brokenness, low self-esteem, hatred, abandonment, brokenness, guilt, loneliness, unworthy and so much more. I begin to scream out and I didn't care who was looking at me; I didn't care who was talking about me, what they were saying about me or what they thought about me because it was just me and God at that point.

It broke - the wall was broken, and I had no idea how to react; I couldn't breathe and felt helpless! In that moment all I could pray in my heart was, "I need you,' and it was at that very moment I felt God's loving arms surround me. I heard that same small gentle voice say, "Ranae, I'm here, and as the tears are flowing down your face, you're creating the river of your heart. Flowing from you are all the feelings and people that you've held hostage for so many years. Ranae, it's time for you to see yourself the way that I see you. So yes, cry, let it go, let it flow out. As you're emptying your heart with everything that shouldn't be there, I'm refilling it with more of Me -more love, joy, peace, happiness and self-worth. Ranae', today is your day of deliverance!"

I stood there, cried, yelled and screamed and gave all of it to God. When I opened my eyes, to my surprise, I was at the altar face down. I thought I was standing at my seat. Now how I got from my seat to the alter, is beyond me, but when I got up from the altar, I felt so much better. God begin to lead me to people who had felt the same as I did and began to let me see and feel their hearts. He allowed me to minister to them and they begin to fall at the altar one by one. "Ranae," Pastor Grain said, "please take the mic and say what God has lead you say, don't be afraid." Very hesitant I took the mic and begin to say, "Brothers and Sisters, God loves us all and He wants you to know that He's here on today; this is a day of new beginnings for us all. We always hear people say that you don't have to leave here the same way that you came but actually a lot of us do. Many of us do that because truthfully some of us want to, some of us don't know how to let it go and some of us are not honest about what we're facing and going through. There are many reasons why we leave the same way and many of us ask time and time again, "God why did you allow this and why aren't you helping me?" He's saying to us on today, stop picking and choosing what we want to give Him; it's time to open up and give Him everything. He needs us as the body of Christ to be whole and go out and help others. It's time for us to open up our hearts and let Him heal every pain, every anger, every bitterness, every un-forgiveness, every lack, every sickness, every disappointment."

God's words continued to flow out of me like a never-ending spring as I continued to share. "He wants us to stop breaking chains, because when you break the chains the shackles are still attached. Many of us find out that over time, those chains begin to mend back together but God wants all of us to be completely free. God wants all of us to start unlocking every chain that the enemy has over our lives, our family's lives, our children's lives, our finances and health. In order to unlock something, you need a key and the key is the word of God that He's placed inside of you. It's time for all of us to begin to speak those things that are not as though they were. It's time for us to start using our keys. When you stick a key in a lock, the chain and the shackles are still bonded together but they both fall off. The chain that connected heart ache and pain doesn't have to hold you down anymore, use your key. You want healing, take out your key… Isaiah 53:5 says,

'But he was wounded for our transgressions, He was bruised for our iniquities; The chastisement for our peace was upon him, And with his strips we are healed'.

You want peace, take out your key. 1 Peter 3:11 says,

"Let him turn away from evil and do good; let him seek peace and pursue it.'

Whatever it is, take out your key and begin to speak and unlock. Unlock every chain the enemy is trying to hold over you. And once you're free, go and help free someone else. Show someone else how to speak and unlock. The only way for you to be bound again by the same thing you were free from, you literally would have to pick it up and clamp it back on yourself. Begin to speak and loose.

By the time God was finished speaking, everyone was at the altar; six people gave their lives to God, fourteen rededicated their lives back to God, and seven join the church family. I began to look around for my kids and saw them in the back of the church ministering and praying for other children. After church, Pastor Grain called me into his office and said "Ranae, you don't know proud I am of you; my wife and I have been praying for you for such a long. Thank you for finally listening and taking heed to the voice of God." He continued to say, "all of us appear to be good on the outside but we have hidden hurts and pains that we refuse to let go of on the inside and because of that, we are damaging our flesh. Today was a day of releasing and we all needed it. I looked at him with tears still in my eyes and said, "Pastor Grain, I had a true encounter with God on this week, and despite all the hurt that I endured, I got exactly what I needed, true FREEDOM!" First Lady Grain asked if she could pray with me before I left and I agreed. After the prayer I left their office to find my children. As soon as I opened the door I was greeted by none other than Veronica Tatum. "Ranae," she said, "today was a good day. I knew something was wrong with you but today had to happen." She continued, "by the way, did Leonard tell you what happened to Diane last week? And before you say anything, let me just tell you, I wanted so badly to be delivered from this addiction of mine but you know how you can say that you want something and you make up in your mind that today is the day and you take that step to go to the altar for prayer, well I did just that. I took that leap of faith and went up for prayer but somehow I didn't get the right person at the altar today to help me with this problem of mine and that chain is still connecting gossip and busy body to my wrist." "Veronica," I said, "you are way too much but I love you anyway," and walked off. As soon as I opened the door to go outside, I saw my children standing by the car. I immediately unlocked the doors so the kids could get in. Jr. asked, "are we ready to go now?" Standing at the door of the car, I glanced over at the doors of the church and gave the biggest smile because I was finally leaving better than I came. "Yes baby," I replied, "let's go home!"

Ending Statement

Every time the enemy attempts to throw obstacles in your way, remember you have the power to speak and loose. Greater works shall we do.

About the Author

Antonya Y. Ballard, a native of High Point, NC, was born on January 2, 1980. She was raised by her grandparents the late Wilbert and Queen Huntley along with her 2 sisters and her brother. Antonya graduated from Ragsdale High School in Jamestown, NC in June of 1998 and attended Davidson County Community College where she obtained an Associate Paralegal Degree. She has also spent some time studying at Eastern Theological Seminary in Lynchburg, VA. She is currently completing her studies in Medical Office Administration – Healthcare Administration. With her continued studies, she is looking to merge them into the Cooperate Legal field concentrating in Healthcare.

Antonya is an ordained Evangelist called to the 5-fold ministry to impact and advance the kingdom of God. Antonya is a prophetic speaker, who has a heart for the youth and young adult and brings a powerful and radical message of deliverance. Antonya has been gifted by the grace of God with a charismatic anointing to impact generations. Antonya is on a kingdom move for God and will not stop until she pursues the purpose God has for her. She loves the Lord and knows that it is only by His grace that she has come thus far and his mercy, which will lead her on. Her greatest desire is to serve God and be an agent of change wherever she may go.

Antonya is the mother of 3 beautiful children: De'Andre, KeShaun and Kierra Ballard. Antonya is also an advocate for the youth/young adult as well as an awesome motivational speaker, who has spoken at many youth and young adult conferences, women conferences, and Sunday morning services. She enjoys edifying and encouraging the body that there is a place in God that shakes the kingdom of darkness and unleashes the Power of God. s

It is her desire to inspire, and lead others through the journey of deliverance by being the blueprint and syllabus for others.

To connect with Author Antonya Ballard for

engagement requests please email or call:

fierybeaconcpg@gmail.com

Phone: (302) 404-3973